LITTLE CAPTAIN
Claudio Muñoz

Mini Treasures
RED FOX

A Red Fox Book

Published by Random House Children's Books
20 Vauxhall Bridge Road, London SW1V 2SA

A division of Random House UK Ltd
London Melbourne Sydney Auckland
Johannesburg and agencies throughout the world

Text and illustrations © Claudio Muñoz 1995

1 3 5 7 9 10 8 6 4 2

First published in the United Kingdom
1995 by The Bodley Head Children's Books

First published in Mini Treasures edition 1999
by Red Fox

Printed in Singapore.

RANDOM HOUSE UK Limited Reg. No. 954009

ISBN 0 09 928174 0

Aren't boats wonderful things?
    Lucien could watch them for ever sailing
in and out of the harbour.

And Grandad knew lots of stories about sailing. He had once been a sailor himself.

One day at the market Lucien found an old
model boat. Many years ago it had belonged
to another child, who had thrown it away
once it became old and shabby.

They took it home and repaired it. How
different it looked with its new colours
and that very odd set of sails! (Those were
the only spare bits of material Grandma
could find.)

Lucien was delighted and, for no particular reason, decided to call it The Star.

But what was Grandad doing?

Wait, Lucien, don't look yet!

That evening Grandad gave Lucien a little wooden figure. It was a handsome little captain with a black beard, in a blue uniform and white cap.

After Grandma and Grandad kissed him goodnight, Lucien looked closely at the little figure. It seemed to look back at him.

And that night he held the captain tight as he snuggled down to sleep.

The next day, Lucien had hardly
finished his breakfast before he
ran down to the river with the
boat and its captain.

The Star sailed beautifully
and Little Captain stood high
on the deck. A noisy
seagull appeared
above them.

Was it saying something to Little Captain?
I don't know, but The Star turned and began
to sail away, following the seagull. Lucien
ran along the bank and shouted, 'Stop!' and
'Come back!' until the boat, captain and
seagull turned a bend and he could see them
no more.

Down the river sailed The Star and Little
Captain, the seagull always in front.

Under willow trees and bridges, past fields
and quiet villages; then the river widened
and they streamed by boatyards and
warehouses, big buildings
and massive ships...

...until they reached the open sea.

Little Captain followed the seagull
towards ominous dark clouds.
Astonished sailors watched
them brave the storm.

Then in the distance a lonely figure
waved and shouted, adrift on her broken boat.

Oh, the disappointment
when she saw it was only a toy!

But she never saw Little Captain
make a dash for the cabin...

...or disappear inside the broken radio.
She never knew that he repaired it so that
she could now call for help.

But worst of all she never knew
that Little Captain was trapped
and couldn't get out at all.

Then the rescue helicopter roared
overhead and the lonely sailor
was lifted up to safety. Down
below, her boat smashed against
the cliffs. Help had come just
in time.

The sailor held on tightly
to The Star. 'My lucky star,'
she sighed.

Look at poor Lucien.

All day he searched the river bank in vain. Little Captain and The Star seemed to have vanished.

Grandma and Grandad tried their best to cheer him up. But it wasn't easy: they were quite sad themselves.

The news that evening showed pictures of a sea rescue. The woman interviewed was holding The Star!

'Lucien, she's got it!' Grandad rushed to the phone.

Was Little Captain there? It was hard to tell.

Some days later the sailor called in. She gave The Star back to Lucien, saying, 'I'm sorry the little captain is lost. I feel sure he helped me, though I'll never know how.'

Lucien tried hard not to cry, but managed to say, 'Thank you'.

Was there any hope of ever seeing Little Captain again? He was going to miss him.

The holidays were over. One lovely autumn day after school, Lucien went to play on the beach.

His dog bounced
happily in front and
chased a seagull.

The seagull stopped and
where she stopped the
dog began to dig.

At the bottom
of the hole, damp
and scratched, Lucien
found Little Captain.

In bed that night Lucien held Little Captain tight, right close to his ear. 'Now you can tell me what really happened,' he whispered. And Lucien closed his eyes and listened to the story...